❋ CONTENTS ❋

Chapter 1

WINTERTON

For the last fifty miles, I don't think I stopped smiling for even one second. That's because my mum and dad and I were driving up to Winterton.

"How much longer?" I asked my dad.

He smiled. "Didn't you just ask me that, Tess?" he said.

"That was a long time ago," I replied. "At least ten minutes."

"We've still got a while to go," Dad said. "At least another hour."

"I hope we don't hit any traffic," my mum added.

We live in River City, but we're not from there. We think River City is too crowded, too busy, and too dirty. I guess that's because until last summer, my family lived in Winterton.

Winterton is a tiny town. It only has one café and one shop. It's cold all year round. The first snow is usually in October. My dad says that's why it's called Winterton, because it's a town where it's always wintery!

In fact, there's only one reason most people ever go to Winterton. That reason is Craggy Mountain, the best skiing and snowboarding mountain in the county.

Growing up in Winterton, I learned to snowboard almost before I could walk. Snowboarding is my favourite thing in the world.

My best friends Sofie and Anna and I used to snowboard every day. After school, we'd go straight to the mountain and snowboard all afternoon right until teatime. Some weekends we hardly did anything other than snowboard!

The best part is we all got to ride for free. All of us had a parent working at Craggy Mountain Resort, so our ski lift tickets were always free.

This year, though, both of my parents got new jobs down in River City. So we had to move. It was really hard for me to leave Winterton.

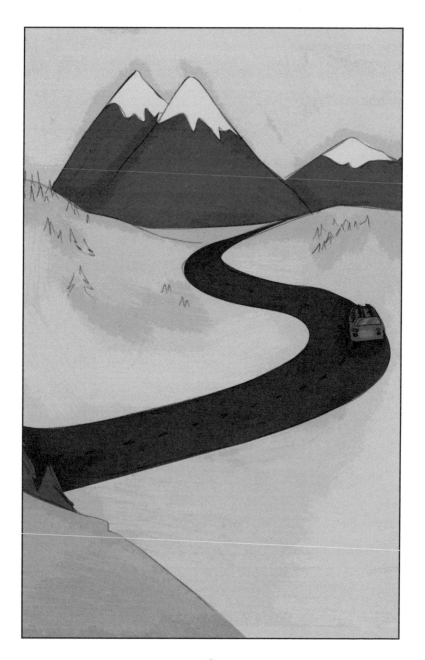

I made my parents promise to take me back to Winterton every winter for a week.

Now we were almost there. I couldn't wait to see my best friends and hit the slopes.

Chapter 2

REUNION

My dad pulled our car into a parking space at the resort. "Finally!" I said. He had hardly stopped the car before I opened my door.

I grabbed my board and boots from the back of the car. Then I headed towards the lodge to change into my snowboarding clothes.

"Don't go too far!" my mum called out. "And be careful!"

"Meet us back at the lodge for lunch at one o'clock!" my dad added.

"Okay!" I called back with a smile.

For a moment, I glanced around the lodge, looking for Sofie and Anna. I pulled my mobile phone from my pocket, but there was no signal.

I shook my head. "Stupid mountain," I said to myself. "Always blocks my signal."

After one more look around, I sat down on a bench to put my boots on. In a few minutes, I was all set.

I put my board under my arm. Then I headed towards the ski lifts.

I was sad that I hadn't seen Sofie and Anna. But they didn't know I would be there. I was planning to surprise them.

Every winter, Craggy Mountain Resort has a snowboarding competition called the CMR Cup. Anyone can go in for the Cup in their age group, but one of the employees' kids always wins.

It makes sense. Kids from the city just don't get to practise as much as kids who live in Winterton.

I don't like to show off, but I won four years in a row. Sofie came in second every time.

This winter, I made sure my parents planned our week in Winterton so I could compete again. I wanted to be the first kid from River City to win – even if I hadn't lived there very long.

I got in the queue for the lift to the top of the mountain. Just then, I heard my name.

"Tess?" a voice said. "Is that you?"

I turned around and saw Sofie and Anna coming out of the lodge.

"It *is* her!" Anna said.

Anna was smiling like crazy, but Sofie wasn't looking at me. She was looking down at the ground.

"Hi!" I called back, waving. I gave up my place in the queue to run over to my friends.

"I can't believe you're here," Anna said. She glanced over at Sofie.

"Hi, Tess," Sofie said. She tried to smile, but I could tell she wasn't really happy. She still wouldn't look me in the eye.

"Hi, Anna. Hi, Sofe," I replied.

My good mood was starting to fade. To be honest, I was expecting a happier reunion than this.

"I'm here for the whole week," I went on. "That means I can compete in the Cup!"

Anna looked at Sofie again. "That's great, Tess," Sofie said. "Really."

Then she turned around and went back into the lodge without saying another word.

Chapter 3

LEFT OUT

"What was that all about?" I asked Anna.

"I'm not sure," Anna replied. She tried to smile. "I'll go and check on her."

Anna quickly chased after Sofie. I picked up my board and tried to keep up. By the time I got through a small crowd and into the lodge, I couldn't see them anywhere.

I sat down on a bench near the door and looked at a nearby clock.

It was already 11:30. I didn't have much time before lunch with my parents.

After a few minutes, Sofie and Anna walked over. I stood up.

"Is everything okay?" I asked. It was weird to feel so out of touch with my friends. Something was obviously going on, but they didn't want to tell me about it.

"Yes," Sofie said. "I just had to, um, go to the loo."

"Well, should we go for a few runs?" I asked.

"Sure," Anna replied. She smiled at me, and I smiled back. At least Anna seemed happy that I was back in Winterton.

Soon we were on the three-person lift up to the top of Craggy Mountain. I felt the cold mountain wind blow across my face.

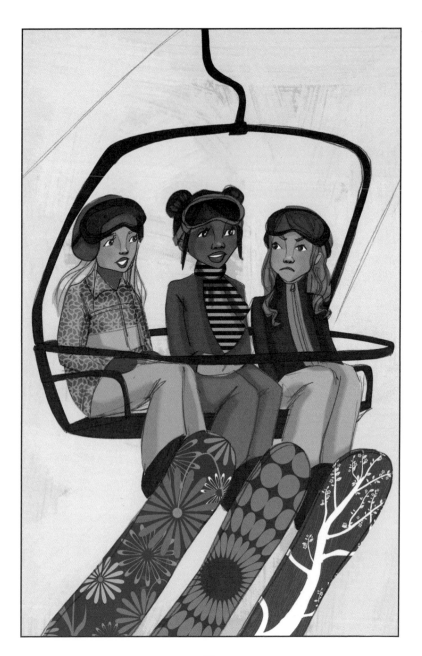

The air got even colder as we glided higher and higher up the mountain.

"I have missed this so much," I said, smiling.

"You've only been away for, like, five months," Sofie said. "It's not like you've been gone for five years or something like that."

I didn't know what to say to that, so I looked at my hands. "I just missed it," I said quietly.

The ride to the top of Craggy Mountain is pretty long. But when your best friend is giving you the cold shoulder, it feels like it takes about a million years to get to the top.

Finally, I saw the peak. "Here it comes," Anna said.

I turned and smiled at her. I was glad she sat between Sofie and me on the lift. It would have been even harder otherwise.

As the lift reached the drop-off spot, I stood up and let my board take me off the lift. The three of us glided a few feet. Then we stopped in a place where we wouldn't get in the way of other skiers or boarders.

From the top of the mountain, you can choose a few different routes. Some are fast and steep, and others are a little slower.

"Which way should we go?" I asked.

Sofie shrugged. "Doesn't matter," she said without looking at me.

Anna looked at Sofie, then at me. She smiled and said, "Yeah, you should choose, Tess. You've been away, after all."

"Okay," I said.

I looked up at the trails sign. I wasn't sure which one to choose.

"She can't even remember the different choices," Sofie said. I frowned. She was acting like I couldn't hear her.

"You know, I'm standing right here," I said.

"Whatever," Sofie said. "Just pick a trail so we don't freeze to death."

I stared at Sofie. She didn't look back. I felt myself starting to get very upset. Instead of getting into a fight with Sofie, though, I just picked a trail.

Without a word, I pushed off and glided to the top of Conifer Run. I clipped my back foot into the board and started down. I didn't even care if Sofie and Anna were behind me or not.

Chapter 4

QUICK RUN

I had a good run, but it wasn't as fun as I'd hoped it would be. I wasn't even thinking about snowboarding. Instead, I was too busy feeling sad about Sofie.

I had no idea why she was so angry with me. I hadn't seen her since July. I couldn't have done anything wrong.

When I reached the bottom, I turned to look for my friends. They weren't in the queue for the lift.

After a few minutes watching people reach the bottom of the run, I still couldn't spot my two friends. I kept looking for a while, but I didn't see them anywhere.

The big clock over the lift line said 12.30. I was supposed to meet my parents in half an hour.

"I guess I have time for one more run," I thought.

I got back in the queue for the lift. Soon I was soaring over the trees on my way back to the peak.

About halfway up the mountain, I spotted Anna and Sofie below me. They were on Hairpins and Needles, one of my favourite trails.

"They took a different trail," I thought. "Probably so they could talk about me."

When I reached the top, I realized I only had about ten minutes before I was supposed to meet my parents at the lodge. They hated it when I was late for things.

"Guess I better take Straight Shooter," I said to myself. That trail was the quickest way down.

Soon I was flying down the slope. It's pretty much a straight line from the top to the bottom.

Of course, you can't just go straight down the whole way. Your speed would be way too high!

Instead, you have to cut back and forth the whole time. But you still go pretty fast.

I got to the bottom in good time. When I stopped, a spray of snow shot out in front of my board.

Even though my friends were being weird, I couldn't help smiling and feeling good. I was back in Winterton on my board!

I quickly took off my board and ran into the lodge. It was 12.55.

"And I even have five minutes to spare," I said to myself. Then I spotted Anna and Sofie eating lunch.

I walked over to my friends. Right away, I turned to Sofie. It was time to get to the bottom of this.

"Hi, Sofie," I said.

She didn't reply. She just kept looking down.

"Look," I went on, "obviously you're cross with me about something."

"No," Anna said. "She's not. Don't worry, Tess."

Just then, my parents walked over to us.

"Hello, love," my mum said. "Hi, girls."

Anna said hello, but Sofie just sat there. Now she was just being plain rude. "Hello, Sofie?" I said.

Finally she turned and looked at me. "Just go back to River City, Tess," she shouted. "Okay?" Then Sofie got to her feet and stormed off.

Chapter 5

LUNCH

My favourite food in the entire world is the macaroni cheese at Craggy Mountain Resort's café. But that day, I barely touched it. I just poked at it with my fork and leaned on my fist.

"You're pretty cheesed off with Sofie, eh?" my dad said.

I just shrugged.

"Try not to let her ruin this week for you, love," my mum said.

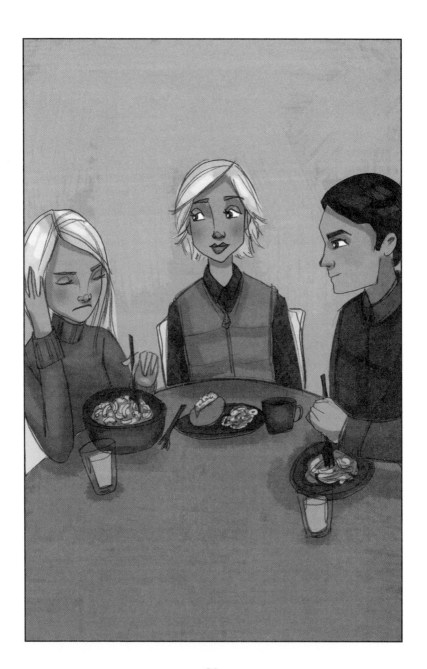

"I won't," I said. "I don't even care, really."

"You don't, huh?" my dad asked.

"No, I don't," I replied. "I only wanted to come up so I could compete in the Cup anyway."

"Hmm," my mum said. "If I remember right, you haven't even mentioned the Cup recently."

"That's right," my dad added. "You've only talked about Anna and Sofie for the last month, since we started planning this trip."

Maybe that was true, but I didn't care anymore. For the rest of the week, I planned to just snowboard and think about the Cup.

My appetite started coming back. The macaroni cheese was as great as ever.

"Remember, sweetheart," Dad finally said after a few minutes of silent eating. "Sofie was your best friend for years."

"I know," I said. "So what?"

"So," Mum replied. My parents always talk as a team like that. They like to finish each other's sentences. "So maybe she's a little angry at you for leaving Winterton."

"It wasn't my choice to leave!" I replied. "That's dumb."

"Maybe," Dad said. "But sometimes people get upset over dumb things."

I looked down at my food. I wasn't hungry anymore.

Chapter 6

SITTING OUT

Sometimes I'm happy when I'm right and my parents are wrong. This time, I wasn't happy.

The next morning, I found Sofie and Anna at breakfast.

The café has a great breakfast buffet. Piles of fresh fruit, scrambled eggs, and all kinds of yummy sausage and bacon and stuff. It's a good way to start a long day on the slopes.

"Hi, Anna," I said. I joined them in the queue for the buffet. "Hi, Sofie," I added quickly.

"Good morning, Tess," Anna replied. Sofie, of course, didn't say anything.

"Sofie," I went on, "I know why you're cross with me."

She spun and faced me. "Oh, do you?" she asked. "Why am I cross with you?"

"Because I moved to River City," I said. "But I didn't want to move. I would rather have stayed in Winterton with you lot forever."

Sofie just glared at me. Then she dropped her tray and stomped off towards the loo.

"I guess my parents were wrong," I said to Anna. "They said she was hurt because I moved away."

"Nah," Anna said. "We know you had to move because of your parents' new jobs."

"Then what is it, Anna?" I said. I felt desperate. "Why is Sofie so cross with me?"

Anna glanced at the toilet door to make sure Sofie wasn't coming back. She wasn't, so Anna turned towards me. "You know how you win the Cup every year?" Anna asked.

I nodded. "Of course," I replied.

"And Sofie always came in second every year?" Anna asked.

Again, I nodded. "Yes," I said.

"Well," Anna went on, "when you left, of course we knew we would miss you. But Sofie also realized she had a great chance of winning the Cup this year."

Then I realized what was going on. "So, with me here this week," I said, "Sofie thinks I'll win again."

Anna nodded. "She pretty much thinks you came back this week just so she couldn't win," Anna said.

"That's crazy!" I said. "I would never do that!"

"I know you didn't do it on purpose," Anna said. "But Sofie isn't so sure."

That's when Sofie walked over. "Are you talking about me?" she asked.

"Yes," I said. "Sofie, I didn't come back to take the Cup from you."

Sofie looked at me. Her eyes were soft, like she'd been crying. "You didn't?" she asked.

"Of course not," I said. "I thought it would be fun to be in the Cup with you two again, that's all."

"Well, it will be, I guess," Sofie replied.

No one said anything. We were probably really holding up the line for the buffet.

"Listen," I said finally, "I won't even enter the Cup."

"What?" Anna said.

"You won't?" Sofie asked.

I shook my head and reached for the bacon. "Nope," I replied. "I'm going to sit this one out and cheer for my friends Sofie and Anna."

I moved down the queue and filled my plate. The next thing I knew, Sofie threw her arms around my neck.

"Thank you, Tess!" Sofie said. "I really appreciate it."

Well, we were friends again. We ate breakfast together and spent the rest of the day making run after run on our snowboards.

I watched my friends as they shot down the slopes. Sofie had really got better at her jumps and tricks. She even pulled off a perfect 360.

It was nice that no one was angry at anyone else. But by the end of the day, I felt sort of empty inside.

The truth is, I really wanted to enter the Cup.

Chapter 7

SIGN UP

After a few days, I was starting to feel really sad. I mean, I was happy to see my friends again. I was especially happy that Sofie wasn't angry at me anymore. That had been the worst feeling.

But it seemed like we had just switched places. Sofie was having a great time now. She was smiling all the time and having a lot of fun on the slopes. It was nice to see her so happy.

Meanwhile, I was hardly trying at all on my snowboard. My tricks were pathetic, my speed was slow, and I wasn't really having fun.

Early on Friday morning, the day before the competition, we headed over to the half-pipe. That's a long ditch on the slope for doing tricks.

Anna and I sat on the edge. We watched Sofie take a run through the pipe.

"Sofie has been practising on the pipe a lot, huh?" I asked. I could tell from her tricks that she'd been working hard. She was landing much better than she used to. She seemed much more confident.

"Constantly," Anna replied with a nod. "She spends all afternoon on the pipe after school."

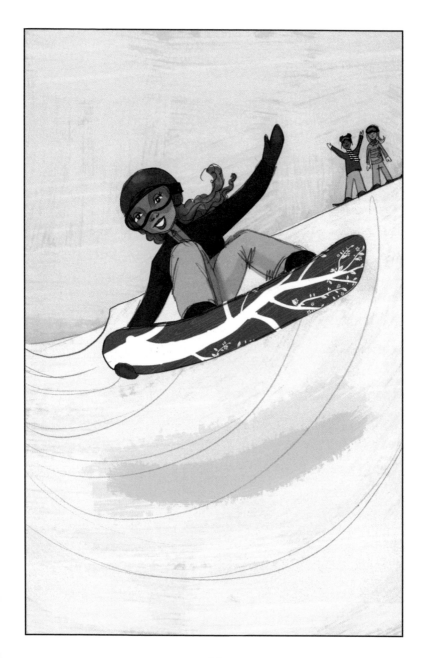

"What about you?" I asked.

Anna shrugged. "I prefer the downhill, I guess," she said. "It's cool."

We watched Sofie take one last trick off the lip. It was a perfect 360 with a front grab. I was impressed.

Sofie made the landing perfectly and then slid out of the bottom of the pipe. Anna and I coasted down to meet her.

"That was great, Sofie," I said. "You're so much better at the half-pipe!"

"Thanks," she replied. Then she looked at the big clock over the chair lift. "We'd better get to the lodge," Sofie said, turning to Anna. "We need to get our names on the list for the Cup."

"Oh, yeah!" Anna said. "Sign-up starts at ten this morning."

The two of them turned and glided towards the lodge. I watched them for a minute.

"I can't believe I'm not going to be in the Cup," I muttered to myself. Then I turned and followed my friends to the lodge.

By the time I got to the lodge and took off my board and helmet, my friends were standing in front of the sign-up list. I walked up and stood behind them.

"There," Sofie said, putting down the pen. "I'm ready for the Cup."

Anna picked up the pen and scrawled her name on the sign-up list. "Me too," Anna said.

Sofie nodded. "This will be my year!" she said happily.

Then Sofie turned and saw me standing behind her. She took a breath and sighed. "Tess," Sofie said. "This is dumb."

"What is?" I asked. For some reason, I couldn't look her in the eye.

Sofie laughed. "You know what," she said. I felt her arm around my shoulder.

"I was being a big baby," Sofie went on. Then she said to Anna, "Give me that pen."

Anna glanced at me, and I shrugged. She picked up the pen and handed it to Sofie.

"Thank you," Sofie said. Then she scribbled something on the sign-up list. "There."

"What did you do?" I asked. I looked over her shoulder. She had written my name on the sign-up list!

"Sofie!" I said. "But I promised not to be in the Cup this year."

"I know," Sofie replied. She picked up her helmet and snowboard. "But like I said, that was dumb."

I smiled at her. "Thanks, Sofie," I said. "And to be honest, you're so good on that half-pipe now, I'm pretty worried about my chances anyway."

Sofie laughed. "Then we'd better get out there and practise," she said. "You don't want to embarrass yourself."

Chapter 8

DOWNHILL RACE

The Cup began on Saturday morning. The bottom of the slope was covered in different coloured flags to show where the different groups should gather. My group's flag was yellow and had a big "11 to 13" on it.

There were ten girls competing in our group. Of course, we knew most of the other girls. They had all been at Craggy Mountain since we were little.

There were a few girls we didn't know. We thought they were probably from River City. I wondered if someday I'd know them better than I knew Sofie and Anna.

A woman walked up to our flag. I recognized her from the last season.

"Hi, girls," she said. "I'm Angie, and I'm in charge of your group for the Cup."

"Hi, Angie," we all replied at once. A few of us giggled.

Angie leaned towards me. "I'm glad to see you here, Tess," she said. "Can't have the Cup without our champ!"

I smiled. "Thanks, Angie," I said.

"Okay, so as most of you know," Angie said, "the Cup is two events. A downhill race, and the half-pipe."

Angie looked at the clock. "We'll be doing the downhill first, in about ten minutes," she said. "So get loosened up, get your gear on, and get in the queue for the lift."

Anna raised her hand. "What trail are we running?" she asked. "I mean, for the race part."

"Hairpins and Needles this year," Angie replied. "Should be a good race!"

Soon, the ten of us, and Angie, were at the top of the mountain.

We were all set to start the race. We were lined up on a thick black line that had been painted right on the snow.

"Remember, the girl in first gets five points," Angie went on. "Second place gets four points, and third place gets three points."

"What about the pipe?" asked one of the girls I didn't know.

"The pipe will be scored by the judges," Angie said. "The highest possible score is five. So the total score to aim for is ten."

"What did you get when you won last year?" one girl asked me.

I know I blushed then. "Um, I got 8.8," I said.

"Tess is the best on the mountain," Sofie said, throwing her arm around me.

I shook my head. "Not this year," I said.

"Okay, girls," Angie said. "Let's go!"

We all cheered.

"On your marks ... ," Angie called out, " get set ... go!"

We all shot off the starting line.

Hairpins and Needles is one of the trickiest trails on Craggy Mountain. It's full of really sharp turns and sudden steep drops. I love it.

Around the first curve, Anna, Sofie, and I were really close. At one point, we could have reached out and grabbed each other's hands. We reached the first jump at the same time and launched together.

"Woo!" Anna called out. Sofie and I laughed.

"We're winning!" Sofie called out. I could hardly hear her over the rushing air and the sound of our boards on the snow.

It was a great run. But before long, we reached the top of the last steep drop. The finish line was at the bottom. I could see a small crowd gathered around.

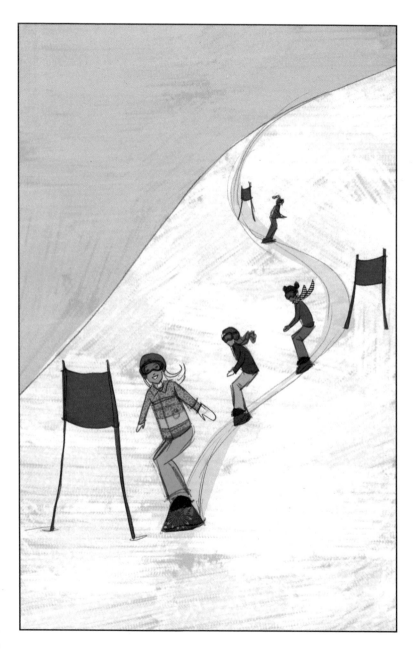

I leaned and cut sharp into the snow. I'm usually faster on these downhill races than Sofie and Anna.

I glanced over my shoulder. Sofie was close behind me, and Anna was close behind her. I saw a few other girls coming over the last lip, not far behind Anna.

In a split second, I was across the finish line. With my arms in the air, I cut sharply to stop, sending a spray of fluffy snow in front of me. Sofie and Anna finished right after I did.

A voice crackled over the slope loudspeaker. "In the girls 11 to 13 group," the voice said, "the winner is last year's Cup champ, Tess Harris, with five points!"

Sofie and Anna were at my side. They each gave me a high five.

"In second with four points, Sofie Waller," the voice went on, "and that's three points to Anna Moore for third place."

"Good job, Tess," Sofie said. "But watch your back on that half-pipe!" she added with a smile.

"Oh, I will," I replied.

The truth was, I didn't even care about winning. For the first time since I came back to Winterton, we were all happy.

Chapter 9

THE PIPE

We took a break for lunch (with lots of hot chocolate). Then the girls from our group met with Angie at the top of the half-pipe.

"Here's the fun part, girls," Angie announced. "Time to really show off."

"Who are the judges?" a girl asked.

Angie pointed at a long table near the bottom of the pipe. There were four people sitting at the table.

"Those are the judges," Angie said. "They are the head of the patrol, the head of the ski school, the winner of last year's adult Cup, and the owner of the resort."

Sofie whistled. "Wow," she said.

"Yeah, they're a good group of skiers and snowboarders," Angie said. "They definitely know their stuff. So do your best out there!"

With that, Angie called out the first to hit the half-pipe. It wasn't anyone we knew well.

The girl dropped into the pipe and started her routine. She didn't fall or anything, but none of her tricks were hard.

"Boring," Sofie whispered to me and Anna. "You have to try tougher tricks than those."

The judges took a few muments, then showed her score: 2.5. Not bad, but not good enough to win.

Anna went next. She must have really listened to Sofie. She went for a 360 on her very first trick.

She made it, but almost fell. Sofie and I cheered like crazy.

"Well done, Anna!" I called out.

After her turn, the judges held up a 3.1. We went crazy cheering.

"She beat her score from last year," I pointed out.

Next it was my turn. I hopped over to the top of the pipe.

"Whenever you're ready," Angie said with smile.

I pulled on my goggles and clipped into my board. Then, with a nod to Angie, I dropped in.

Right away, I pulled off a smooth grab with a lot of air. The landing was perfect.

On the next trick, I decided to go for a 360. But I wobbled on the landing, just like Anna had.

I guess I was a little out of practice from being in River City. After all, there's not a mountain there that I can practise on every day.

To end my run, I pulled off a couple of clean 180s and then glided out the bottom of the half-pipe.

After cutting into a stop, I turned to face the judges and pulled off my goggles and helmet. I knew I'd done okay, but not great.

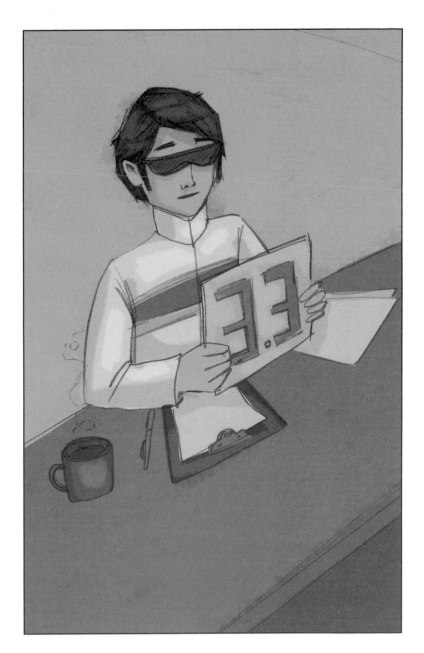

The judges lifted my score card: 3.3. That wasn't as good as last year's score.

Still, it was pretty good. To beat me, Sofie would have to score better than a 4.3. I was pretty sure she could do it.

A few more girls took their turns. Sofie went last on the pipe. The highest score in our group had been 3.5. That meant Sofie's turn in the pipe would have to be pretty amazing.

From the bottom, Anna and I watched her drop in. She hit the first trick with a lot of speed.

"Wow," I said. "She wasn't even doing her best the other day, huh?"

Anna shook her head. "Nah," she said. "That was just for fun. She's really amazing on the pipe now."

And she was. Sofie's first trick was a 360 front grab. She did it perfectly. Everyone cheered like mad.

She did trick after trick. She didn't wobble. She looked confident. She just kept impressing us.

Once, she got so much air she was able to grab the back of her board and pull it up almost to her helmet. It was amazing.

When Sofie came out of the pipe, it sounded like the whole resort was cheering for her. Anna and I certainly were!

It only took about a second for the judges to hold up their score card. Sofie got a 4.9!

"Sofie!" I called out, running over to her. I threw my arms around her neck. "That was amazing!"

Sofie hugged me back. "Thanks, Tess," she said, smiling. "But I'm just glad you were here to be with me."

I smiled back. "Me too," I said.

A voice crackled over the loudspeaker. "With a record score of 4.9 on the pipe, and a total score of 8.9 for the competition," the voice said, "the winner for the girls 11 to 13 group is Sofie Waller!"

Angie came running over. She was carrying the trophy.

It was the same one I got to hold up for the last few years. But not this year.

"Congratulations, Sofie," Angie said. "I've been watching you on the pipe this season. You really deserved to win." She handed Sofie the trophy. Then she walked away.

"You really did deserve to win," I told Sofie. "Even with me in the Cup too."

"Thanks for making sure I worked that out," Sofie replied.

Sofie took my hand and held the trophy up. The crowd cheered. It felt like they were cheering for me too.

ABOUT THE AUTHOR

Eric Stevens is studying to become an English teacher. Some of his favourite things include pizza, playing computer games, watching cookery programmes on TV, cycling, and trying new restaurants. Olives are one of his least favourite things.

ABOUT THE ILLUSTRATOR

When Tuesday Mourning was a little girl, she knew she wanted to be an artist when she grew up. Now, she is an illustrator who is especially keen on working on books for children and teenagers. When she isn't illustrating, Tuesday loves spending time with her husband, who is an actor, and their son, Atticus.

GLOSSARY

compete try to win

confident have a strong belief in your own abilities

embarrass make someone feel awkward and uncomfortable

half-pipe U-shaped ramp with a flat section in the middle

lift device that carries skiers or snowboarders up a mountain

lodge hotel at a ski resort

recognize know who someone is

resort place where people go for rest and relaxation

reunion meeting between people who haven't seen each other for a long time

MORE ABOUT SNOWBOARDING GEAR

Would you like to learn how to snowboard? Here's what you will need.

* **A BOARD.** Check out ski shops in your area. If you're looking for something cheaper, try searching online or in your local newspaper for a used board – you might find a great board for less cash.

* **FOOTWEAR.** You will need special snowboarding boots. They can be expensive, so a good pair of boots is another thing to look for in second-hand shops. You'll want a high-quality pair to keep your toes warm and safely secured to your board!

* **GOGGLES.** Going fast down snowy slopes can make the icy wind really dry your eyes out. Goggles will help keep them moist, and keep the snow out of them.

* **BINDINGS**. These keep your boots strapped to your board. Buy them wherever you buy your boots.

* **OUTDOOR CLOTHING**. You're going to be snowboarding in lots of snow – you'll need to stay warm! You will want to be wearing salopettes (ski trousers). You'll also want a snowboarding jacket, which is longer than a traditional ski coat. To make sure you're comfortable, wear lots of layers under your outerwear.

* **A HELMET**. This isn't necessarily required, but you'll feel more comfortable knowing your head is safe.

* **GLOVES**. Snowboard shops sell them, but you can buy gloves anywhere – as long as they're waterproof.

If you prefer, you can hire most of these things at resorts or online.

DISCUSSION QUESTIONS

1. Why was Sofie upset when Tess returned to Winterton? What else could Tess have done to find out what was wrong?

2. What are some good ways to cope when you or a friend move away? How can you stay in touch while you're apart?

3. At the end of this book, Sofie wins. What do you think would have happened if Tess had won? How would the story be different?

WRITING PROMPTS

1. Try writing chapter 3 from Sofie's point of view. What does she think and feel? What does she hear and see?

2. Pretend you're Tess. Write a letter to Sofie and Anna after you leave Winterton and return home to River City after the CMR Cup.

3. What do you think happens after this book ends? Write another chapter. What happens next?

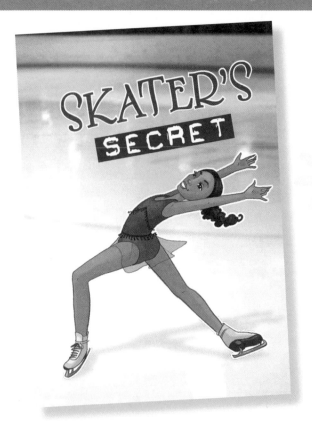

Maggie and Shannon are sisters. They both do figure skating but Maggie is really tired of Shannon always being in the spotlight. Maggie is determined to come out from behind her sister's shadow. How can Maggie learn to shine, when Shannon always knows exactly what she is doing?

Lately, Marissa's heart hasn't been in her dancing. She feels clumsy and awkward, and being bigger and taller than the other girls doesn't help. Marissa doesn't even bother trying out for the part of Rose Fairy in the coming recital. Can anyone persuade her that a dancer's spirit is more important than how she looks?

FIND OUT MORE

Books

Extreme Snowboarding, Blaine Wiseman
(Weigl Educational Publishers, 2009)
Snowboarding, Andy Horsley (Ticktock
Media, 2009)
Snowboarding **(To the Limit series)**, Paul
Mason (Wayland, 2008)

Websites

www.snowboardclub.co.uk/learn
This website from Snowboard Club UK
has lots of information about learning to
snowboard.